Tortoise
Races Home

by Jill Atkins

Illustrated by Beccy Blake

First published in 2009 by
Franklin Watts
338 Euston Road
London
NW1 3BH

Franklin Watts Australia
Level 17/207 Kent Street
Sydney
NSW 2000

Text © Jill Atkins 2009
Illustration © Beccy Blake 2009

A CIP catalogue record for this book is available
from the British Library.

ISBN 978 0 7496 8516 4 (hbk)
ISBN 978 0 7496 8522 5 (pbk)

Series Editor: Jackie Hamley
Editor: Melanie Palmer
Series Advisor: Dr Hilary Minns
Series Designer: Peter Scoulding

Printed in China

Franklin Watts is a division of
Hachette Children's Books,
an Hachette UK company.
www.hachette.co.uk

Rabbit, Squirrel, Mouse and Tortoise were playing in a field.

Soon, it was time
to go home.

4

"I'll race you all home," said Tortoise.

The other animals
laughed. "You're too
slow," they said.

"I'll win," said Rabbit.
"I can run fast."

11

"I'll win," said Squirrel.
"I can jump through
the trees."

"I'll win," said Mouse.
"I can roll down the hill."

15

Tortoise laughed.

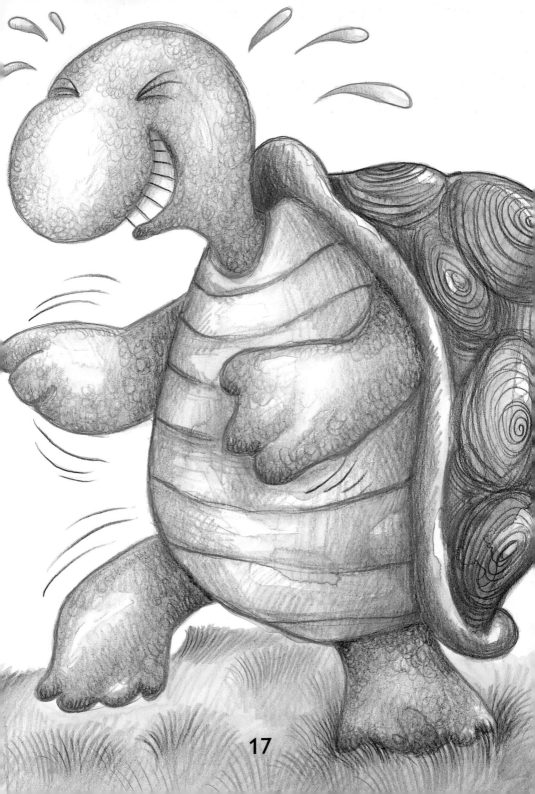

"No," he said.
"I'll win ...

… because I'm home already."

And he popped
into his shell!

Puzzle Time!

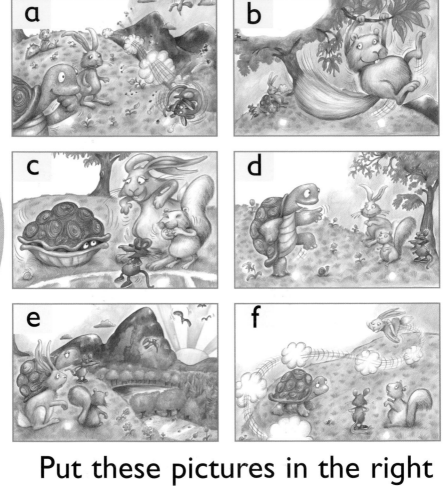

Put these pictures in the right
order and retell the story!

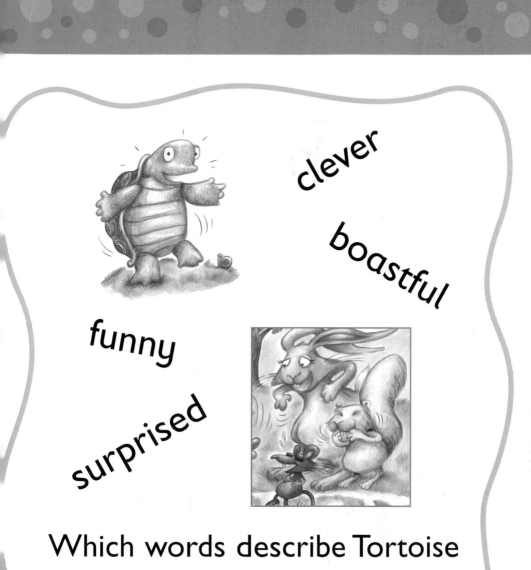

clever

boastful

funny

surprised

Which words describe Tortoise
and which describe the
other animals?

Turn over for answers!

Notes for adults

Answers

Here is the correct order!

1.e 2.d 3.f 4.b 5.a 6.c

Words to describe Tortoise:
clever, funny
Words to describe the other animals:
boastful, surprised